ADAPTED FROM CHARLES DICKENS'

A Christmas Carol

ILLUSTRATED BY CHRIS McDONOUGH

MODERN PUBLISHING
A DIVISION OF UNISYSTEMS, INC.
NEW YORK, NEW YORK 10022

benezer Scrooge was the meanest, stingiest man in the world. He paid his loyal clerk, Bob Cratchit, barely enough to live on and he kept the office so cold that poor Bob Cratchit sat at his desk and shivered all day long.

On Christmas Eve, Scrooge's jolly nephew came to wish him a Merry Christmas, but Scrooge could only frown and grumble, "Bah, humbug!"

That evening when Scrooge returned to his dark and
gloomy house, he was startled to see that the brass knocker
on his door was transformed into the face of his long-dead
business partner, Jacob Marley. He stared at the face
for a moment, but then exclaimed, "Bah, humbug!"
And he went inside.

Scrooge did not believe in ghosts, but even so, he checked under his bed, in his closets, behind the curtains and up the chimney. Then he double-locked his bedroom door and went to sleep.

Minutes later, Scrooge awoke to a clanking, clattering racket. He peeked from behind the bed curtains and standing right beside him was the ghost of Jacob Marley wrapped in heavy chains. "You must change your ways, Ebenezer," Marley's ghost warned. "You will be visited by three spirits, listen to them… and learn!"

The first ghost to appear was the Ghost of Christmas Past. She took Scrooge back in time and reminded him that he was once a happy and loved young man. He had friends and family that filled his life with joy. "Please take me away," Scrooge begged the spirit. "I don't want to see any more of this!"

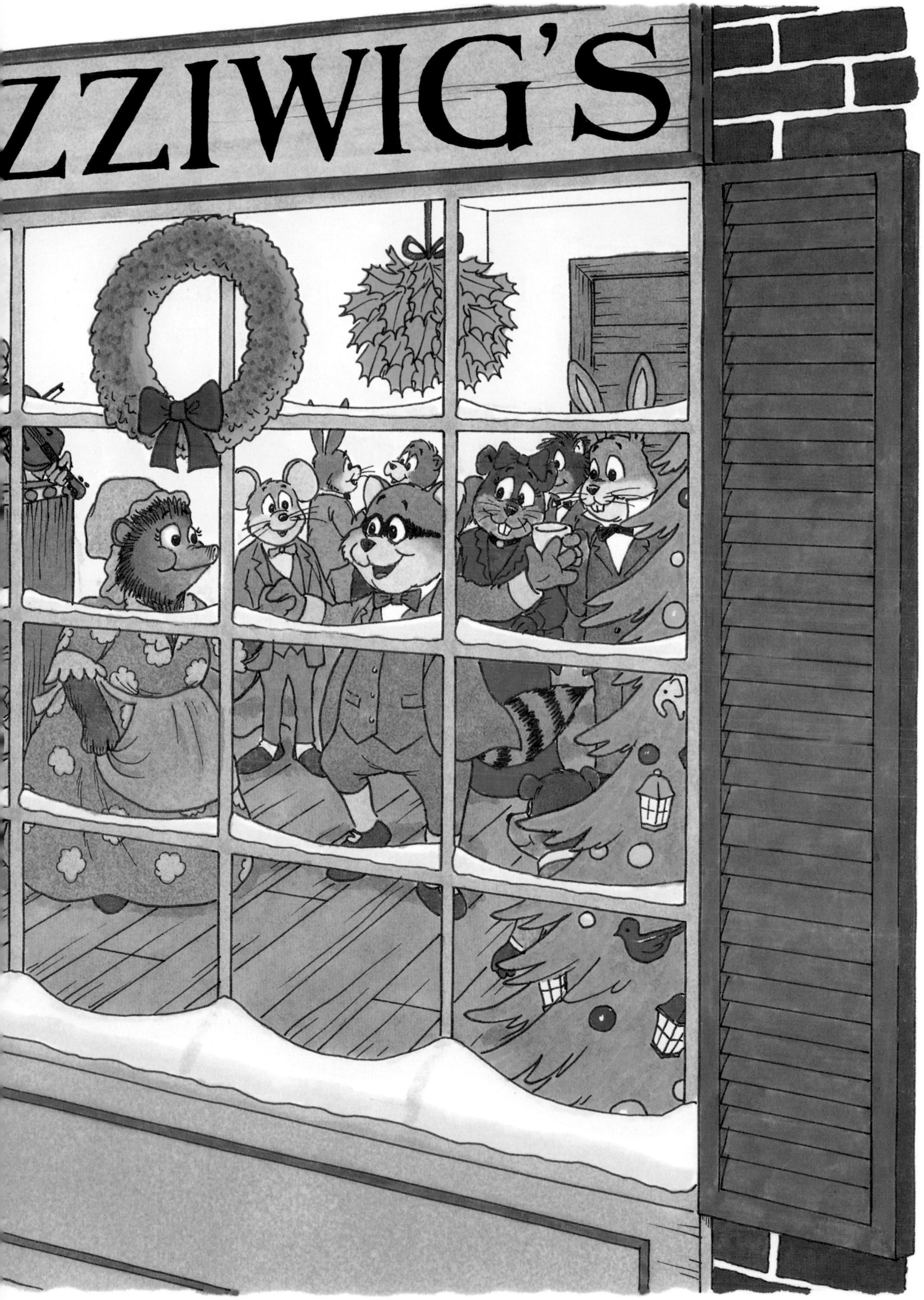
ZZIWIG'S

No sooner was Scrooge back in his bed, than he was awakened by a brilliant light coming from the next room. He slowly crept into the room and there he saw a magnificent throne made of many foods. On top of the throne sat a royal giant. "Who-oo-oo are you?" Scrooge asked, trembling.

"I am the Ghost of Christmas Present!" the giant roared.

Scrooge held tightly to the spirit's robe and off they flew over the streets of London. "Where are we going?" gasped Scrooge.

"You shall see!" replied the mighty giant. Finally, they stopped at Bob Cratchit's house and watched the joyous family give thanks for their Christmas dinner.

"God bless us, everyone!" Fragile Tiny Tim exclaimed.

Scrooge stared at the tiny crutch leaning up against the wall. "Will Tiny Tim live another year?" Scrooge asked.

"Not unless things change," the spirit answered.

Scrooge was soon dropped back into his bed and before he knew it, a black-shrouded spirit appeared before him. This was the Ghost of Christmas Yet to Come. Scrooge was so frightened by this sight that he pulled the covers over his head trying to hide from the spirit. But the spirit approached him and beckoned him to follow.

First they flew over Bob Cratchit's house where the family was mourning Tiny Tim's death.

Then the spirit brought Scrooge to his own grave to witness his own funeral. No one was there. No one even seemed to care that Scrooge had died. "No!" cried Scrooge. "I don't want to die this way. I will change! I will honor Christmas in my heart and I will keep the Christmas spirit throughout the year."

When Scrooge awoke it was Christmas Day and he was a new man. He jumped out of bed and flung open the windows. "Merry Christmas!" he cheered. "Merry Christmas to everyone." Scrooge reached into his coin purse and threw coins onto the streets for all the children.

Scrooge sent a huge turkey to Bob Cratchit's house.
He then went to visit his nephew and stayed for Christmas
dinner and was always a welcomed guest from that day on.

Soon afterward, Scrooge gave Bob Cratchit a raise and he helped to get Tiny Tim a special doctor. Before long, Ebenezer Scrooge became known as a good friend, a good master, and as good a man as the good old city ever knew!